Where Is God?

Poems, Short Stories and
Random Thoughts

ROBERTO ALAGO

This is an original work of the Author.
Published in USA

All rights Reserved.
© 2022 Roberto Alago.

The partial or total reproduction in any form or format is prohibited without prior consent of the publisher.

Roberto Alago
6904 Vesta Brook Dr.
Morrow, GA, 30260

Table of Contents

Dedication 6
Personalize Your Copy 9
Nothing 10
God Made Them All 13
The Atlantic Garden's Master 21
Thirty One 23
Where is God? 27
My vow to you... 34
27th Anniversary 37
Avalanche Encounter 39
My Father; The Inventor 43
Fishing Paws 51
Spiders On My Truck 55
Getting Married 61
Bitcoin; Herald of The New World Order 65
Sister Odell's Pumpkin Crunch 70
Tragedy in our schools 73

Dedication

I dedicate this book to
God All Mighty who gives
the inspiration and to my sister;
María Luisa Alago for instilling
in me the love for poetry.

Personalize Your Copy

From our childhood we are told we are not supposed to write on the pages of a published book. It is this Author's belief that reading and writing is an experience best enjoyed when shared between writer and reader. Therefore, we have left enough spaces on the pages of this book to allow you the opportunity to personalize your copy. Enough space to make your own annotations.

On those spaces, you may write your own thoughts and feelings. You may also illustrate what you are reading. Whatever it is that reading these passages bring to your mind from your memories or your inspiration. Write your own parables, poems, prayers, stories or thoughts. It is your space; use it and enjoy it.

Nothing

This song came to me on a Sabbath morning in the year 1994 in South Korea during family worship, before leaving the house for Church. It is our tradition to sing the song that each family member wanted to sing. When it was my son Jorge's turn to pick a song, I asked him; what do you want to sing? He answered very seriously; "Nothing".

Realizing that the Child was being rebellious; I knew, whatever I said next, would set the tone for the rest of the day and this service was either going to be a blessing or a curse for my family. So, I skipped him and asked my son David; what do you want to sing? He answered with a grin; "Nothing". So, I asked my son Ruben and he gave me the same answer. I knew they really wanted to sing. They were just trying to follow their big brother.

I elevated a silent prayer to God and asked for help. When I opened my mouth, I started singing the following song. The smiles and laughter that followed are still a precious memory. Everyone liked it and asked for it to be sung over and over.

Now this song is part of our regular family worship service. The original version is this one, in English. During a Pathfinder Club Camp meeting of the Forest Park, GA, Central Spanish SDA Church, I translated it to Spanish and it was well received by all members.

I hope it is the blessing to you and your family that it has been for mine and the countless young people that have sung it at various camps and Pathfinder activities throughout the years since its creation.

For an audio version, follow this link to my webpage where I'll be glad to sing it for you.

https://robertoalago.com/nothing

You may also download the music sheet from my website.

Nothing

Nothing, nothing, nothing.
Nothing is the song.
Nothing, nothing, nothing,
nothing can go wrong.

Because Jesus loves you,
Nothing can go wrong.
Because Jesus loves you,
Nothing can go wrong.

Nothing, nothing, nothing.
Nothing is the song.
Nothing, nothing, nothing,
nothing can go wrong.

This poem, I wrote for my daughter Liza, when she was a little girl, inspired by another poem of the same name. That she may know, God made everything for us to enjoy, because of his love for us...

God Made Them All

God made them all; great and small.
The lion, the tiger, the bug and the spider.

God made them all; great and small.
The dogs and the fleas, the lakes and the seas.

God made them all; great and small.
The plants and the trees, the birds and the bees.

God made them all; great and small.
The fish and the whale, the breeze and the gale.

God made them all; great and small.
The moon, the sun so far, the twinkling little star.

God made them all; great and small.
Down on earth, up in the sky,
God made them all, I will tell you why.

God made them all; great and small;
Thinking of love. This, my child is true.
God made them all; because he loves you!

After hearing of the death of my friend Antonio Porfirio Candelaria, whom we affectionally called Poncho, I asked God to give me words that would bring comfort to his loved ones. This is the result of that prayer.

Today I cried

Today, as seldom happens in my life,
in the face of my friend's death, I cried.
Was my cry out of fear? I think not.
For death, you see... is everyone's lot.

The common man as well as the king;
are born like the rushing wind;
ignoring when will be the day,
death crosses their pathway.

Just like my friend, just like the wind,
against death's grip, man cannot win.
You and I will someday meet this fate,
probably too early, rather than late.

Unfulfilled dreams we'll leave behind,
our Children to keep us in their minds.
Have courage, don't mind your fate,
because, with death, you have a date.

Poncho's life was taken fast and too soon.
He's life trophies all gathered in a room.
To remember the blessing he was to them,
and to say good-by, to the truest friend.

To live selfishly would be meaningless.
From Poncho, we learned others to bless.
For a selfish person, dear Poncho was not;
he blessed our very lives, a whole lot.

So, if tomorrow when I am gone,
you wonder, the reason for my cry.
I'll tell you... to a dear friend, I said good-by.
That is why today, I cried.

Once, at Southside Church in Jonesboro, GA, I heard the preacher say; "not everyone measures success in the same way". In an instant the words for this poem began to run through my mind...

How Do You Measure Success?

We all measure success ...

The lion, by catching a prey,
and the prey, by running away.
The constructor, by building up,
and the bomber, by blowing it up.

Jesus, by giving you a crown,
and Satan by making you frown.
The arsonist, by starting a blaze,
the fireman, by the blaze quenched.

The hit man, by taking a life,
the physician, by saving a life.
The pilot, by a safe landing,
the derby driver, by a wrecking crash.

The businessman, by expanding,
the homeless, by food in the trash.
The artist, by a new painting sold
the collector, by the art when is old.

I, by the love of my children, yes!
And You?
How do you measure success?

My home town was recognized by our former Mayor (Carlos Mendez) as the Atlantic's Garden. On one of my trips home, while walking by my old school, I came across a childhood friend. She told me a lot of things, one of which was that she was dying of AIDS.

Knowing how little time she had, I told her about God's love for her and about His willingness to forgive. Right there, on the sidewalk, we prayed and with tears in her eyes she asked for God's forgiveness. Once home, I wrote her name vertically and wrote this acrostic prayer...

The Atlantic Garden's Master

Good Lord; the Atlantic Garden's Master.
Reach out; revive that sad looking flower.
In that solitary corner, she sits every hour.
My… how was she stepped on and mistreated.
In an instant, she lost her radiant beauty.
Lord, please… restore her inner beauty.
Do not let her forget that you love her.
Awake her to know, you are still her Master.

When I was in South Korea, I had several soldiers under my supervision. Among them, there were two women. One of these returned from her vacation, very depressed, the night before her birthday, because her husband had asked her for a divorce. In the morning she told me what was happening in her life. At that moment I did not know what to tell her,. So, I suggested she talk to a counselor.

Later, while I was praying, I asked God to give me some words to tell her, that would help her reflect on the blessings of life, rather than the bad and also to cheer her up. This poem was the result of that prayer. After writing it, I put it through the bottom of her bedroom door. She found it upon her return, read it and heeded to the advice.

The next day, she arrived in the office all radiant and happy. I asked her how she was feeling. She said that the night before she had followed my advice and, for the first time in a long time, she had prayed and thanked God for all his blessings. She had a good night sleep and had awakened in the morning feeling refreshed.

A few weeks later she showed me an advertisement for a poetry contest. I entered the contest with this poem and it was published in the anthology "Dance on the Horizon" In its original version, it had five stanzas but the contest had a rule limiting the poem to 20 lines. So, I shortened it to these twenty lines and now, can't remember the missing ones.

Thirty One

Today you're thirty one.
I hope you have lots of fun.
Thirty one is not that bad.
Some… thirty one never had.

I have no other gift for you.
These words, are the best I can do.
But I want you to know tonight.
God loves you, with all his might.

Blessings He gave you under the sun.
Start counting, the love of your son.
He gave you health to do your duty.
and garnished you with great beauty.

So tonight, when you hit the sack
and before you lie on your back,
don't forget, get down and pray,
thank Him, for all He blessed today.

This poem came about on a day where bad news was the order of the day. In the morning news they were talking about homes being destroyed by the elements. On one side of the country, there was rain, while in others there were forest fires and on the internet I got news of a father questioning God about his child's poor health. I got caught up in the moment and questioned God about these things. He made me understand that, yes in this world we will be afflicted. But, we are not alone. God is with us. He sees our pain and gives us comfort. He also gave us each other; to support one another.

Where is God?

Where is God,
when the sea goes raging into my home?
Where is God,
when the wind plays sticks with your own?

Where is God,
when the fire takes everything you work so hard to obtain?
Where is God? Can He see the pain?

Where is God,
when the earth quakes and delivers a crushing blow?
Where is God,
when your child is sick from an unseeing foe?
Where is God,
when the ones you love, are forever gone?
Where is God?

Where is God,
when you know soon, you too will be gone?
Where is God? Does He care? Do you know?

Where is God,
in the midst of human suffering?
Where is God,
when you are confused, sad and lonely?

Where is God,
when all you have is despair?
Where is God?... Oh where? Where?

God is at your side, every step of the way.
God is in the morning sun,
that warms and brightens your day.

God is in the birds,
that fill with music your broken heart.
God is at your side, every step of the way.

God is...
in all who give up their own blessings,
that you may be blessed instead.

God is in the physician, that helps ease your pain.
God is in the rescuer that saves the day.
God is at your side, every step of the way.

God is in the friend,
whose words give you comfort.
God is in the man
or woman that lends a helping hand.

God is in the little child
that smiles and brightens your day.
God is at your side, every step of the way.
Yes! Every step of the way.

The following poem I wrote after returning from the funeral of three dear elderly friends. I also wrote a similar poem in Spanish called "Tres Mariposa" (Three Butterflies) that is published in my book ¿Quién es Dios? (Who is God?)

Three Caterpillars

Once there were three helpless eggs.
They knew not, and were not.
They had no dreams, no worries,
not a care in the world.

Then, three caterpillars they became.
They ate, they toil, they loved
and were much loved.
Until… They grew grey and old.

Until the day they left their cocoons.
Then to The Creator they came,
the reward for their lives to get,
and their beautiful wings to claim.

Rejoice ! Rejoice! Rejoice, I say.
Those three common looking caterpillars,
have reached the pinnacle of their existence,

Three butterflies they now are.
Reunited with our loved ones we will be;
those three who went before us
and are so special to you and me.

To Alicia, Gilberto and Leonor
We said, not good-by. But, see you later.

For someday, sooner than later,
We will also leave our cocoons.

Leaving only a token of our essence.
We will happy with the outcome be.
For in the blink of an eye…
in our God's presence,
Three Butterflies we will see.

Every time there is a mass shooting or similar crime, politicians try to find the solution to the problem in the law. However, not everything can be fixed by passing more meaningless laws; specially, not man's heart. For that, we need the only solution and that is God.

If God is in ma's heart there will be no law required, because the natural response of a man with God in his heart is to love his neighbor and love does not do evil. After such an event, and hearing all the politicians going back and forth about gun control laws. I wrote this poem… It's silly, I know. But, so are all those who thing that by taking away the tools, the killers will suddenly stop killing.

Let's Outlaw People

When all the rifles have been confiscated…
People will die by handguns.

When all the handguns are confiscated…
People will die by cutting weapons.

When all the cutting weapons are confiscated…
People will die by bats, rocks and other blunt objects.

When bats, rocks and other blunt objects are confiscated…
People will die by the hand of other people.

You see…We've known all along…

The problem is not in the weapons.
The problem is in the heart of people.

So, let's outlaw, people killing people.
Wait a minute! That's already against the law.

It's in every code everywhere.
It's even in the Bible. Yes. But…

The Bible has been outlawed.
So… What can we outlaw now?

I know… It's simple!
Let's cut to the chase.
Let's… outlaw people.

In 2011, after being on the road for four and a half months as an 18 wheels truck driver, I returned home with a new set of wedding rings, and in a family reunion I made the following vow to my wife:

My vow to you...

First, I want to thank our Heavenly Father for giving me the blessing of a wonderful wife and for giving us the privilege of rearing such great Children. Certainly, I have done nothing worthy of these wonderful blessings.

Second, Emilcen, my love...

Today, August 6th 2011, before our Children and Grand Children, with this ring, I, Roberto Alago Hernandez, promise to love, be true and save my self only for you, as long as we both shall live.

I make this solemn vow, not only in the presence of these witnesses, but before God Almighty and His Holy Angels. May they help me keep my word and help me to love you as God does, because you deserve such love; for being a good wife and an excellent mother to our Children.

I do pray to God that, as the circumference of this ring has no beginning nor end may our love endure forever. For I believe, that long before we were born, you were pre-destined to be my wife. May we remain in his love, for all eternity.

As these two shiny groves, may God grant us to stand together against all odds and circumstances, may we remain true and our love be strong in sickness and in health, for richer or poorer and if He wills that we be touched by death, may we rest in peace, side-by-side, to be awaken together at His return.

May these three horizontal stripes be a constant reminder that we owe our love to the will of God; The Father, The Son and The Holy Ghost, that we belong to Him and we are under His constant watch and His loving care.

As a testament of our love, may our descendants be as the endless number of vertical lines on this ring. By this, the universe will know that God is love and he rewards those that love Him and each other.

May God grant us that our descendants live and walk in beauty, good health, safety, peace, wisdom and wealth. Above all, may they remain in His love, love for God and love for each other. That they may grow in the knowledge of God and the assurance that, one day we will meet with Him, to receive the reward of His eternal love.

Emilcen, my love... Because, I do love you and can't imagine my life without you; with this ring, I make you my friend, my lover and my wife forever.

Now I must ask you... Emilcen Sayago Rodriguez, AKA Emilcen Alago,

Do you accept this prayer, these blessings and this ring?

(She Said... Yes!)

In 2010, for our 27th Wedding Anniversary I wrote…

27th Anniversary

I went to dig for diamonds to Arkansas
leaving at home, my most valuable treasure.
The most beautiful woman, I ever saw,
whom long ago, I married with pleasure.

Like it was only yesterday, it seems,
we were married in the city of Atlanta
by a crossed-eyed justice of the peace
before whom we committed with ease.

Intimate friends came, to wish us well;
the bride's sister was there as well.
The groom looked sharp in military garb.
The bride was happy cause she had my heart.

So... today while for diamonds I dig
and in the mud I look and work like a pig.
I think of my beautiful bride,
whom long ago, was looking so bright.

At your side my love, I wish I could be.
Your name and mine to write on a tree.
I pray to God, this wish he grants:
that soon I'll have you in my arms.

So... for now... good-by I must say,
to my wife at whose side I wish I could stay.
Upon my return from this back braking task
to tell her "I love you", whenever she asks.

Here is a little bit of fiction I wrote for the Public Radio's eighth season of the Three-Minute-Fiction Challenge. Didn't win but, it was fun to write. Yes, it is a work of fiction but, also helps us understand that God works in mysterious ways and will do whatever it takes to protect his children...

Avalanche Encounter

She closed the book, placed it on the table, and finally decided to walk through the door. Grabbing her skies, she heads for the hills. On the lift, she strikes a conversation with Mark, whom rides with her. At the top, they say their goodbyes and part ways. She selected her favorite trail, puts on her skies, unrolls her hat into a facemask, zipped her jacket, and puts on her safety goggles and gloves. Seizing her poles and leaping up and forward she alights.

Since she was beginning to increase in speed, she maneuvers to control her rate of descent and to avoid some obstacles. She approaches an older woman that was just standing on her path. With a terrified look, the woman pointed with her right index finger to the top of the hill and yelled: ava-a-la-a-anch!

Hilda took one quick glance behind her and immediately realized she was in mortal danger. She knew, no one could outrun or survive an avalanche of that magnitude. There wasn't much time. She had to find refuge and fast. Clenching her poles, she began to thrust forward, while at the same time maneuvering around obstacles and looking for a safe place to hide. But, where was it?

She kept going down the hill, with the wind buzzing in her ears, faster and faster. Her arm and leg muscles tensed up. Her vision became very acute and focused; almost like a tunnel and time seemed to have slowed. Only seconds had elapsed. But, to Hilda, it felt like an eternity. Frenetically, she looked and looked and could not find that perfect hide out, to save her life. She began to hear the roar of the skiers Grimm Reaper, closing in behind her; and that's when it happened...

Right in front of her, a door opened and a ramp was laid before her. Without wasting any time, she headed straight for the ramp. As soon as she was on board, the spaceship started to ascend, the ramp was retracted and the door closed. Hilda was so glad to have survived that she had not noticed where she was. She removed her gear, got up from the floor and began to look around. Still breathing hard, she began to absorb in her mind what had transpired in the last few seconds.

She begins to move around and when she sees what looked like a commercial airplane window, she took a peak and saw planet Earth getting smaller and smaller. Soon she realized; she was in space. Every science fiction movie she ever saw came to her memory. Her mind was working on high gear, going through all the possibilities. She began to wonder...

What did the Aliens look like? What were their intentions? Where were they going? Why did they choose to save her and not any of the other skiers that by now lay buried beneath tons of snow, rocks and debris? When would she get to meet them? Will they be able to communicate? Did they rescue or harvest her? All her questions were about to be answered. She heard some footsteps...

Someone or something was approaching. She could hear her own heartbeat, it was racing faster than when she was on the mountain. She began to have second thoughts about meeting them. What if they wanted to invite her for lunch? What if...She was lunch? She looked for a place to hide and then realized the room was empty. The door opened and soon she met her host... It was Mark!

Welcome Hilda. Have no fear. I came to save you. First, allow me to introduce you to my crew... (THE END)

My Father; The Inventor

If I ever met someone who wondered Where God was in his life and what was He doing; was my father. You see, my father was orphaned at a very young age. After the death of his parents, he went to live with an uncle that was not kind or understanding. At times, his uncle was downright abusive. Still, my Dad did not let his circumstances define him. While He questioned God and at times his faith waivered, in the end he came to understand that God was with him all along.

Despite his circumstances, my father managed to get an education and raised a family. For years, he wasn't the nicest person, husband or father. Yet, little by little he came to know God and learned to trust in him and eventually, accepted the fact that God's ways are mysterious and all things work for good for those who believe and obey God.

My Father was a Master Mechanic and responsible for the invention of many tools, while he was working for the US Air Force. He served in the civil service from 1945 - 1971. He wasn't always a Mechanic; he started out as a Shoe Shine Boy, a Store Clerk and a Carpenter. When Ramey Airfield began construction in 1936, he became a Contractor Carpenter.

While working in the construction of Ramey Airfield in Aguadilla, Puerto Rico, he decided to take advantage of a new on-the-job training opportunity being offered by the Air Force and that's how he became a Civil Servant and a Mechanic, in 1945. He remained at his post until Ramey Air Force Base was closed in 1971.

The Automobile was a new thing on the island and there weren't many Mechanics around. So, I guess we could say my Father was a Pioneer in his field. In fact, by the time I was growing up, every Mechanic in Aguadilla knew my Father. Many would tell me he had been their Teacher and how good he was at his chosen career.

As part of his job, my father used tools on a daily basis. Many times, he would suggest to their tool suppliers a modification or the creation of new tools. Tools that I know he create himself, even though he didn't get the credit, were the "L" shape Flathead Screw Driver, a simple, portable, three screws, Steering Wheel Puller, a Remote Starter Switch, an Amp / Volt Meter combo tester box, the Starter/Alternator Motor Magnetic Tester, and a high beam Flash Light.

Not only did he create them, he had the prototypes in his tool box. Unfortunately, upon his death, one of my brothers inherited his toolbox and sold it. Somewhere out there, is a lucky person holding the original prototype of these tools and probably, don't even know it.

My father's name was Antonio Alago Acevedo and his tools would be marked AAA. If you come across a toolbox full of tools bearing that mark, you may be holding a one of a kind or the first tool off the assembly line; a real piece of Auto Mechanics' history.

As to why he would not seek credit for his inventions, it may have been a combination of factors. You see, he was born in 1918 in the island of Puerto Rico. He was a Mulatto, the Child of a black man and a Taino woman. Back in those days, being a Mulatto, in Puerto Rico, meant you were a third class of citizen. So, he grew up accustomed to not owning property and not being recognized for his good deeds. He was happy, just getting enough to feed his family and staying under the radar of those who would hurt him just for not being white. Don't get me wrong, he was not afraid to fight, to defend himself, if he had to. But, he chose to live in peace and avoid conflict, whenever possible.

His creations, except for the high beam flashlight, were inspired while he was working for the Air Force. So, as far as he was concerned, he had been handsomely rewarded and they belonged to the Air Force. So, he never thought about applying for a patent or seek the recognition he rightfully deserved.

He served until Ramey Air Force Base closed and the Air Force offered him a choice between reassignment to the Continental United States or retirement. Refusing to leave his home town, he opted for retirement.

After he retired he continued to work as an independent mechanic. That's when he really learned to trust in God. There were days when business was good and there were days when he would question the wisdom of having retired. Yet, he and his family were always provided with all the necessities of life; food, clothing and shelter. Not once did his family suffer for needs and God always provided the means by which he would be able to provide for his family.

God is good to those that put their trust in Him. He has promised to provide for all of our needs. All he asks in return is for his followers to be good to one another. Do no harm to self or those around you and be thankful for everything He provides.

At age 65, my father decided to surrender his life to Christ and was baptized by immersion. The Holy Spirit did a marvelous work in him and he stopped drinking alcohol which was the source of most of his problems. He also quit smoking and started to eat healthier. Every day, he would read his Bible and he became totally different person than what he had been. All for the better.

If you decide to follow in his footsteps and accept Jesus into your life, God will help you overcome whatever situation you may be facing. I'm not selling false hope, as some may thing. I'm not saying you will not have problems or challenges in your life. We all have them. What I'm saying is that even in the midst of the worst storms God will be with you to strengthen you and help you overcome.

Tuxedo; Beloved Pet

Children and sometimes adults, question the love of God when their beloved pets die. As I'm sure was the case of my Grandchildren at the loss of their dog Tuxedo.

Few dogs I have met in my life are as friendly and playful as Tuxedo was. While his full name was Tuxedo Quantavious Jackson Alago; we called him Tux; for short.

When my son and his wife rescued Tux from the Cobb County pound, they had gone there to look for a cute little fluffy Maltese or similar canine for my daughter-in-law. Instead, my son fell in love with a two years old Boston Terrier. So, they adopted it, named it Tux and shared their home with Tux for sixteen wonderful years.

Tux was a coddler. Tux enjoyed playing and sleeping with his new pals. Two years later, their first baby was born. They were a bit anxious because, they didn't know how Tux would react. So, they decided to slowly introduced Tux to their newborn. To their surprise, Tux was overjoyed and was super protective of the new baby boy. Tux started sleeping by the baby and later they became good playmates.

Five years later, the second baby was born and Tux took to him as naturally as he did his older brother. When the baby was old enough, Tux and he would spend hours and hours playing, until they were both exhausted.

When Tux was twelve years old, he began to slow down and to experience hearing loss. About this time, Molly; a female mixed breed, became the new family member and Tux's new companion. Surprisingly, it took Tux longer to warm up to Molly than it did to the Children. But, soon they were spending all the time together. Molly's energy is contagious. So, Tux experienced a period of renewed energy; something similar to what a runner calls "a second wind."

Two years later, a beautiful baby girl was born to complete the family and once again, Tux became the perfect playmate and protector; as it did before. They didn't even have a need for a baby monitor; anytime the baby would wake up or cry, Tux would alert everyone.

It truly has been a joy to have Tux as a member of the family. Whenever my wife and I came for a visit, Tux would greet us at the door. Tux's body would be thrusted left and right as if wagging his non existing tail. Whenever we spent the night, Tux would sleep next to my wife. In the middle of the night, Tux would get up, walk around the house, check on all the family members, individually and only then, go back to sleep.

Unfortunately, dogs have such a short lifespan. According to the Vet, Tux outlived most of his breed, as most Boston Terriers die between twelve and fourteen. Tux lived to be sixteen! Only in the last month of his life did Tux loose the will to live.

On one of those rare moments in the life of a pet, Molly seemed to sense something was wrong and laid to sleep with Tux; something she usually did not do. Two days later, Tux would be no more.

Tux is now gone. But, his memory will last for at least two generations. Tux will be remembered as a perfect host, family protector, playmate and above all, a loving family member. Tux will be missed and I'm sure, for years to come, will be the subject of many family conversations. Rest in peace Old Pal. Until we meet again.

Until we meet again? What am I saying? Is there a resurrection for dogs? Some say yes. Some say no. Truthfully, I don't know. I would like to think there will be. If nothing else, is logical.

I mean, if God loves mankind so much, and mankind is so evil… How much more would He love dogs that are so forgiving, loving and loyal? I know the Bible says that in the new Jerusalem there will not be anything unclean and dogs are one of those unclean things. But, the promised of God is that there will be a new earth where we will live and it will be populated with all kinds of animals as it was at the beginning. So, when I'm there I will ask God for my lost pets. I'm sure He has the power to bring them back. Ultimately, if the dogs make it or not, will be up to Him not us.

Fishing Paws

It is common to see a lonely fisherman fishing next to a bored dog or a cat. What is not common to see, is a furry creature working at a commercial fishing outfit. This makes me feel all the more privileged to have experienced this.

You see... in a commercial fishing team there is no room for freeloaders. If you work, you earn your pay. If you don't work, you don't get paid; as simple, as that.

One evening, right after a spectacular sunset, I was just walking along the sea shore on the "Song of the Rocks" beach in Aguadilla, Puerto Rico, when I came across some fishermen that were pulling a drag net. There were three boats in the water and two crews of three men on each rope on the sand. The net was being pulled by the men on one side while the men on the other side just held their position. Suddenly, the last fisherman on the longer line called out to me and said in a rushed tone: "young man, grab that rope" and pointed to the long tail of the net's rope.

Of course, I didn't know what to do and it showed. I had never done this kind of work before. The fisherman looked at me and smiled. He then asked, "First time?" I said "yes." So, he gave me some brief instructions about, pulling at the same rhythm as the other men on the line. Everyone has to pull at the same time or it will not be as easy. He also told me to move up closer to him and to leave the tail end of the rope dragging on the ground.

As both ends of the net were parallel to the shore, all the men began to pull. As the net got closer, it was getting heavier, because of all the fish it had captured. One of the fishermen let out a whistle. Out, from the shadows came running this big, black dog and grabbed the tail end of the rope and began to pull.

That dog was very strong. I sure could feel the difference. With the last pull, all the fish were out of the water and flapping about. The fishermen were quickly picking up fish and tossing them in containers full of sea water, where the fish would remain fresh until taken to the market.

That day, I received my pay in a long string, loaded with fish. When I refused, because, I didn't feel I had done enough to earn it. The fisherman was quick to point out, that according to their way of living, everyone that works, gets paid. I had worked, I had earned it. Then he pointed to the dog and said, "He worked less than you did and he will get his due." His friendly smile, told me that was the end of it and it was useless to continue the argument. So, I picked up my pay, patted my canine co-worker and said my goodbyes.

That day, I learned three very important life lessons:
1. Earning your pay will give you satisfaction.
2. Hard work brings its' rewards.
3. A well trained dog can work just as hard or even harder than some humans.

Later, as I reflected on the matter, I felt sorry for the fish. But, that section of Aguadilla is a fishing village with over 300 families, dependent on fish for their survival. Like it or not, some people still make a living that way. Some families have been doing it for generations and based on the number of boats I saw the last time I was there; it won't be stopping anytime soon. I wish there was an alternative industry we could present our fishermen that is more enticing than fishing. But... What would that be?

We have to take care of our planet, it is the only one we have and we don't really know how much longer humanity will be on it. Oh sure, we always say: "Jesus is coming soon." But, how soon is soon? Nobody knows. One thing is for sure, when Jesus comes, the world will be such a mess; he will take us to heaven for 1,000 years while the earth has its rest and then he will make everything anew. Yes, Jesus is coming soon and he wants you to live on the new earth for eternity. Get ready.

Spiders On My Truck

Working animals and pets share a special bond with their handlers and companions. Often, each can anticipate the actions or reactions of the other. They seem to sense each other's feelings and at times, express joy or sadness in reaction to the other's actions, behavior or mood.

Some animals serve to protect their human companions or their property. Others seem to be content or even happy just being around their human fellows; weather working in an office or just enjoying the trip we call life.

If life is a trip, we need to choose wisely with whom we are going to share our travels and speaking of travels, almost no one on the planet travels more than an Over-The-Road Truck Driver. I soon learned this when I became one.

It was September 2011. I was just fresh out of trucking school and had finished my 6 months of mandatory team driving. I finally was driving my rig by myself and enjoying the solitude. I grew up in a large family, served in the US Army and have a wife, four Children and eight Grandchildren. So, yes, I was definitely enjoying the ride.

I didn't like to admit it but, at times, it felt lonesome. Especially in the mornings, while I was inspecting my truck, before getting on the way. Until one morning; as I was returning from a refreshing and much needed shower. That's when I met her. Spidey, as I named her.

She was huge bird spider. She had created a big beautiful perfect web between my truck and a nearby tree. I stood there just gazing at the perfection of her creation. I was saddened because, I knew that soon, I would be moving out and her perfect web would be destroyed.

So, I talked to Spidey and told her I was sorry that I had to be on my way. As I was almost finished with my inspection, I cranked the engine and gazed at the spider web. To my surprise, Spidey was picking up her web. I continued with the last part of my inspection and lost sight of her.

Before moving out, I looked again. Spidey was gone. I felt a little sad. But, I had work to do and I got on the way. Throughout the day, I thought about Spidey and wonder where she had gone and how she was doing.

At the end of my shift I refueled and parked at a truck stop. Went inside, had dinner and came back to the truck to call my wife. To my surprise, there she was. Spidey had laid her beautiful web between my truck and a light post.

At first I thought, it may be another spider. But, her markings were an exact match. I smiled and welcomed my uninvited guest and told her not to get too comfortable because I was leaving in the morning.

That night, I went out of the truck a couple of times and Spidey was still there. Next day, I followed my morning routine. As soon as I cranked the engine, Spidey started collecting her web. Then I noticed she hid in the mirror housing and that's when I realized, she had traveled in my truck all day the previous day.

This became the routine. Every day I would talk to Spidey in the morning before getting on the way. She would hide behind the mirror. I would drive all day, and in the evening, she would set up her web. I would talk to her some more before going to bed and the next day we would do it again.

One October morning, Spidey did something totally different. Just as I was about to take off, she jumped and walked on my windshield and stood there right in front of me for a little bit and jumped off to the side of the truck. That was the last I saw of her.

Winter came too soon. All throughout the winter, as I drove, I often thought about Spidey and about the way she departed. On how she had stood on my windshield as if saying good bye. We had traveled together through eleven states. We had shared our mornings and evenings. She protected my truck from intruders, as most people would stay clear of a spider web, especially one where a huge spider could be seen. I always parked near a light post to ensure she would get a chance to find enough food.

Is it possible for a human and an arachnid to connect on a spiritual level? Did she understand that I made every effort to make sure she was well fed? Had we become friends? Did she actually say good bye? Or was she just trying to decide which way to go?

Spidey was gone and I was alone again. Winter was over, almost as fast as it came. One spring morning, as I drove, I saw a tiny spider walking out from the back of my truck's mirror. Once it got to the top of the mirror housing the wind carried it away.

57

A few minutes later, I spotted several other tiny spiders crawling from the top of the mirror housing only to be carried away by the wind. The same repeated about four more times. I assumed Spidey had left an egg behind the mirror and now her offspring were moving away. As I was approaching the city of St Louis, MO, I had to concentrate on my driving and don't know if any more spiders had come out.

A few days later, I was at a Truck Stop in Laredo, TX and as I was approaching my truck, I noticed it. It was a beautiful spider web hanging between my truck and the truck on the next stall. In the middle of it was a small spider.

I welcomed it and got into my truck. The next morning, the other truck was gone and so was the spider web. I assumed the spider had hitched a ride in the other truck. I performed my inspection and headed out.

Two days later, while at a company terminal in Dallas, TX. The spider came crawling out of the mirror and set her web and positioned itself in the middle of it. I rolled down my window and started talking to it, as I did with Spidey. I decided to call her, Dallas.

Every morning and evening I would take a few minutes to talk to Dallas. Every morning, as soon as I cranked the engine, she would pick up her web and crawled behind the mirror. Every evening, as I parked, she would crawl out and setup her web once more.

This went on for about six months, then one evening, when I returned to my truck, she was gone. No web, no Dallas. I don't know if she left on her own, like Spidey did before her or if someone or something had scared her. I like to think she left on her own, sensing that winter was soon approaching.

Either way, I feel privileged to have shared over 72,000 miles with my arachnid friends. Up until this experience, I had never thought much about the beauty there is surrounding a spider. Her body is amazingly built and adapted to her environment and way of living. The webs they make are true works of art.

I had seen a spider grow right before my eyes, from a tiny little creature to a full grown and beautiful bird spider. She kept bugs off my truck, kept me company, I provided her with transportation and a new location every day. It was a mutually beneficial relationship. I missed those days of travelling around the country, and I miss Spidey and Dallas. Sometimes I wonder... In the new earth; will there be spiders? Will I ever see them again? Will they remember me?

Getting Married

Wedding; the most feared word in the twenty first century. Not that people don't want to get married, they do. They don't want the stress that comes with planning a wedding and dealing with the aftermath.

Most couples, these days, start their life together having to work extra hours just to earn enough to cover their day-to-day expenses and to pay the loans they took to cover the cost of their dream wedding.

Since I'm writing for an international audience, I would like to ensure I address everyone's cultural differences. In some cultures, the couple getting married is responsible for all expenses. In others, the groom is and in others, the bride. In other cultures, the parents of the couple, the parents of the groom or the bride.

Regardless of your cultural upbringing, if you are paying the bill and want the marrying couple to have a beautiful, once upon a time type of fantasy wedding, save money, and not spend three to five years paying for it, take note.

There are some cultures were the entire community helps the couple by taking charge of one aspect of the wedding entirely or partly. I once planned a wedding for a young couple that were so poor, they only had enough to pay for the license and a small cake. They wanted more. But, couldn't afford it. They asked for my advice.

I suggested, they put their pride aside and ask their closes friends for help. Within a couple of days, their friends had agreed and were happy to cover all the expenses for their wedding; Dress, Decorations, Food, Honey Moon, Limo, Photos, Venue. One friend even agreed to provide the music and entertainment himself. Surprisingly, it was a very entertaining wedding. They had a small wedding with just a few of their closes friends. About, fifty people in all.

Yes, that was for a small wedding but, will it work for a larger wedding? Absolutely, Yes. The next couple I help with their dream wedding had a bigger affair planned. Over two hundred guests, catered food, beautiful venue, a $3,000 wedding gown, bridesmaids, escorts, horse carriage, limo, open bar, Live Band, a DJ, a Wedding Planner and a honeymoon in Aguadilla, Puerto Rico.

All of their wedding expenses were covered and they had one of the most beautiful weddings I have ever seen. They even had four ministers performing the ceremony. Most importantly, they ended up with a little leftover that they put in a bank account to start a college fund for their future Child that was born three years later.

You get the idea. Most people will be happy to help the couple start their lives together, without having to go into debt just to get married. When presenting the idea to your family and friends don't tell them what you want them to pay for. Let them pick and choose from your budget list. Some of the more expensive items, can be paid by more than one party.

Be considerate. Remember that beautiful does not necessarily means expensive. Some people can do wonders for a room with a few flowers and some crepe paper. Why buy two if one would do? Don't buy a $15,000 gown unless you are paying for it.

Planning a wedding is very stressful and full of surprises and last minute happenings. This is where a professional wedding planner will shine. There is not a whole lot they have not seen. Yet, every wedding has its own share of challenges and unexpected issues. Having a Professional on your side will minimize its effects.

Reduce the stress by getting a Professional Wedding Planner. I cannot stress this enough. Don't let a friend or family member take on this job unless you are absolutely sure they are up to the task.

One more thing; Premarital counselling will increase your chances of having a once and for all times wedding. After all, since marriage was invented by The Creator, it is a good idea to seek His counsel and that of your local pastor or priest. Premarital counselling is available at most Christian churches and some community centers around the country. I have heard that even some colleges and universities are offering premarital counselling. Believe me; it is well worth your time. Hope this information was helpful. May God bless your plans and your marriage.

Bitcoin; Herald of The New World Order

Everything comes to an end. Every ending is a new beginning. Bitcoin is no different. The arrival of Bitcoin marks the beginning of an era; One where greed, power and war have no place, one where commerce will be unleashed and the world becomes a village.

For centuries, war has been the daily bread for mankind. Brought about by the greed and power hunger of a few. Every country around the globe has been touched by it. Every lineage has been marred by it. Mankind's development has been curtailed by it.

But, this is a new millennium. People are tired of following a few who only lookout for their own interests. A few that pit us against each other. A few that are willing to go to war over resources; rather than cooperate and have free commerce.

The interesting thing is that the Hebrew prophet Daniel predicted the arrival of Bitcoin and Cryptocurrency in the days of the Babylonian Empire. Now we are seeing the fulfillment of that prophecy.

For years I struggled to understand the prophecy of the prophet Daniel which is recorded in the Hebrew and Christian Bibles in the book of Daniel, Chapter 2 until now.

You see, King Nabuchedenezer had a dream and he was sure it was something important. He had all his magicians, and wise men brought before him to inquire about it and no one was able to tell him what he dreamed and what the meaning of it was; except for Daniel.

The king of Babylon had seen in his dream a statue made up of many metals. The head was made of Gold. The Chest and arms were made of Silver. The Thighs were made of Bronze, the legs of Iron and the feet of Iron and Clay; interlaced but, not mixed. Then he saw a huge stone fall from heaven that destroyed the statue and became a huge mountain.

Daniel explained to the King that the statue in his dream represented his kingdom and every subsequent dynasty afterwards; as follows: Babylon is represented by the head of Gold. It would be replaced by a lesser empire. Just like Silver is not as valued as Gold. That empire would be followed by another, while strong like brass, not as valued as the previous two.

This empire of brass would be followed by an empire that would rule with the strength of iron. Then, in a different twist, when you would expect yet another kingdom or empire, Daniel states that the kingdom of iron would give way to ten kingdoms. They would intermix. But, would not become one; just like the iron and the clay did not mix.

It is in the days of these ten kingdoms that the stone from heaven falls and destroyed the entire statue and all its metals. History is on our side. We can look back and see that what Daniel predicted, happened with uncanny accuracy. All 2,300 years if history!

To make a long story short; historically, we now know that Gold is a good metal to represent ancient Babylon. There has never been another empire as great as the Babylonian Empire. Nor has any government since, amassed as much Gold as they did.

Just like the statue had two arms made of Silver, Babylon was followed by an empire that was ruled by the Meads and the Persians. Medo-Persia never reached the grandiose glory of Babylon and due to the greed and desire of man to amass Gold, Silver was their currency of choice.

The Mede-Persian Empire came to an end and Greece became the strongest empire up to that time. Its strength came from its army with their brass weapons and shields. Brass became very popular in the days of The Greek Empire. India, Japan and China amassed huge amounts of brass and it became the metal that was used to make almost everything for mankind's use: Household goods, jewelry, weapons, etc.

Greece was defeated by the Spartans and became part of the Roman Republic; which ruled with an iron fist. With far more better weapons, that interestingly enough, were made of iron and steel. Iron became the stuff of which things were made; until the end of the industrial revolution.

But, the statue had two legs. Check this out, The Roman Republic became the Eastern and Western Roman Empires. Then, the Roman Empires collapsed and 10 nations took their place. These nations have made many treaties and even tried to develop a commonwealth backed by the Euro. But, as Daniel predicted 2,300 years earlier, they have not become one.

That brings us to our days. We are living in the days when out of heaven falls a stone that was not made by human hands and destroyed the statue and grows until it becomes a mountain. That stone that was not made by human hands and fell is Bitcoin; starting a revolution which will continue to grow until it encompasses the whole world and there is no stopping it.

Here we are, 14 years later. There are, to my knowledge, at least, over two thousand other Cryptocurrency in use today and there may be more to come. Finally, a global monetary system controlled by the masses and not the few. Country after country are discovering and using cryptocurrency. Currently, billions of dollars are invested in Bitcoins and much of it is in circulation. And the beauty of Cryptocurrency is that it serves no purpose to amass it. In fact, it is worthless unless it is in circulation.

It was not made by man's hands because, it was born as an idea of one heavenly messenger named Satoshi Nakamoto, whom, to this date, no one has been able to locate or identify. Like in the days of Sodom and Gomorrah, this heavenly messenger came, did what he was to do and left, without a trace.

Once the whole world is using Bitcoin, the evil greed that has been choking the life out of humanity, will loosen its grip and then there will be a global economy unlike anything we have seen before. A New Order of things in the world. Or, as some have called it; A New World Order.

Cryptocurrency holds no value when hoarded. Unless you put it in circulation, it is as worthless as a meaningless dream. This could only have been divinely ordered. If anyone entity or government tries to hoard it, the people will produce another form it and commerce continues without missing a beat.

Finally, a system that will allow the masses to come out of poverty and there is nothing any government, king or man can do to stop it. Those who try it will be met with frustration, because, like a hydra, when you cut one head, a new one, better and more dynamic, takes its place.
Welcome... to The New World Order.

That's all I'm going to say about that. Take it with a grain of salt. There are many that don't accept this theory. That is OK. Time will tell.

Sister Odell's Pumpkin Crunch

When I was in Hawaii, I used to attend Church at the Aiea SDA Church. There I met sister Odell. She was a Realtor, if memory serves me right. One of the traditions at that church and I hope they still do was; the weekly potluck. Mmmm... just thinking about it makes my mouth water. Every family would bring a dish for their family and enough to serve ten more. Needless to say, the Hawaiians are very generous people. So, the spread was amazing. Food for all and desserts galore.

Every week the same ritual was repeated. The cooks have to be amongst the best in the world. I have traveled extensively and have not enjoyed food so much as I did those two years I spent in Aiea, especially the desserts; cakes, doughnuts, puddings, casseroles, etc. However, my all-time favorite; the one that kept me going back for more, every time it was available, was sister Odell's Pumpkin Crunch; Mmmmm...pure delight.

Words can not do justice. So, I have decided to include her recipe and let you be the judge. On the last Sabbath I was there, I asked Sister Odell for the recipe and she graciously agreed. Not only that, but I told her; "This is so delicious it needs to be shared with the world." She smiled and told me I could share it with whomever I want. So, what follows is Sister Odell's Pumpkin Crunch recipe with few minor modifications I did that I think made the "Perfect" even better.

Sister Odell's Pumpkin Crunch

1 Can (29 oz.) Solid Pack Pumpkin
4 Eggs Slightly Beaten
1½ Cup of Sugar
1 Teaspoon of Salt
2 Teaspoon Ground Cinnamon
½ Teaspoon Cloves
2 (12 Oz. Cans) Undiluted Evaporated Milk

CREAM:

1 Box Yellow Cake Mix With Pudding
1 Cup Chopped Almonds
¾ Cup of Melted Butter

FROSTING:

1 Package (8 oz.) Cream Cheese
1 Cup Powder Sugar
1 (8 oz.) Cool Whip

PROCEDURE:

1. Preheat oven to 350° F.
2. Line a 9 X 13 in. Pan with Wax Paper.
3. Mix Pumpkin, Evaporated Milk, Sugar, Eggs and Spices together and pour into pan.
4. Pour Box of Cake Mix (Dry) over Pumpkin mixture and Put Chopped Almonds on Cake Mix.
5. Spoon Melted Butter evenly over
6. Bake for 50 – 60 Minutes.
7. When a knife inserted comes out clean,
8. Invert into Tray and pull off Wax paper.
9. Spread frosting over evenly.
10. Refrigerate.
11. Cut into rectangular portions.

Go ahead. Give it a try. Let me know what you think. Is this the best pumpkin dessert you ever had or what? If you like it, you can join me in thanking God for the Aiea Church and Specially for Sister Odell. May God bless her, wherever she is. Odell, if you read this, Thanks for Sharing. Every time I have slice of Pumpkin Crunch, it takes me back to 1989 in Aiea Hawaii.

I remember not only the Potlucks, but, the fishing, the services by the beach, the youth and Pathfinders. Everything come back to mind; like a recorded movie. Oh How I love that Church. There, you can feel the love of God. If you have a chance, drop by for a visit; you'll be glad you did.

Stay for the Potluck and tell them Roberto sent you and sends his greetings. It's been over 30 years. But, they are still in my heart. The love of God that brought us together back then, binds us Today and forever. We are a family, God's Family.

Tragedy in our schools

Time after time, tragedy strikes where our most vulnerable are. When our kids can not feel safe at school people ask; Where is God? Well... Remember back in the 80's? People were asking, no... demanding. Yes. People were demanding; the Bibles be removed from the school libraries, that prayer not be allowed in schools. In fact, they demanded that God not be taught in public schools. They even wanted the Ten Commandments, God's Moral law, to be removed from the court houses. So, God, being the Gentleman He is, did as they wished. He stepped back.

See, there is something about God most people don't understand. He is real. He does what He says He will do. He wants to save all mankind. But, He does not force the will. He will not act where He is not wanted or welcomed. He will not Help and ungrateful people. Who in the world is more ungrateful than the people of these United States Of America.

Congress, The President and The Supreme Court have turned their backs to God. Judges are taking bribes and corrupting justice. Teachers have sided with the State and Teach Evolution but, not Creation. They cite Darwin. Yet, Darwin himself believed in God. In fact, in the last line of his book; The Origin Of The Species he states..."But, How it all started? Only God knows."

See that? Even the Champion of the Unbelievers believed in God and he was not afraid to state so. Darwin recognized God. Yet, those whom have been blessed beyond measure by God have turned their backs to Him. How did we get to this? I mean, the existence of God is so obvious that even a Child can see it. Because, the whole universe screams that there is a Creator.

Take the human body for example. More sophisticated than any machine ever designed by man and some want us to believe that it happened by chance, randomly and without any planning. If you analyze the mechanism in a wristwatch, you will conclude that someone designed it. Well, the human body with all of its different systems is billions of times more complicated than a wristwatch and it happened by chance? Impossible.

Just one cell of the human body is many times more complicated than the most complicated machine ever designed by man. And the more we look into to it, the more complicated it gets. Within each body cell, there are many parts and chemicals; Chromosomes, DNA, RNA, Molecular Machines, etc. All of that in one cell and the whole body is made up of billions of unique cells. Each, with their own individual identity markers; kind of an individual address. That was just the human body. What about the Universe?

Consider this… We live in a planet of the solar system, which is one of billions in our galaxy, which is one of billions in the Universe, that is just one of many in the Multiverse. Poof. My mind is blown. Billions and Billions of planets in Billions and Billions of Starts in Billions and Billions of Galaxies all moving in their own orbit for only God knows how long, maintaining perfect order and location and it all happened by chance? No way. It doesn't take a genius to figure out; All of that had to be carefully designed. If there is a design, there has to be a designer. That, my dear reader, is God. His Glory fills the Universe. He is everywhere. Because, He cares about His creation including you and I.

Made in the USA
Coppell, TX
28 November 2022